KEKE'S SUPER-STRONG DOUBLE HUGS

By Elizabeth McChesney and Judy Schiffman

Illustrated by Steve Musgrave

In Memory of Lauri Bauer
and all those parents
whose sudden death has left their children
with sadness but memories of joy.

KEKE'S SUPER-STRONG DOUBLE HUGS

This is a work of fiction. All of the characters, names, incidents, organizations, and dialogue in this novel are either the products of the author's imagination or are used fictitiously.

Archway Publishing books may be ordered through booksellers or by contacting:

Archway Publishing
1663 Liberty Drive
Bloomington, IN 47403
www.archwaypublishing.com
844-669-3957

Because of the dynamic nature of the Internet, any web addresses or links contained in this book may have changed since publication and may no longer be valid. The views expressed in this work are solely those of the author and do not necessarily reflect the views of the publisher, and the publisher hereby disclaims any responsibility for them.

Any people depicted in stock imagery provided by Getty Images are models, and such images are being used for illustrative purposes only. Certain stock imagery © Getty Images.

Interior Image Credit: Steve Musgrave

ISBN: 978-1-4808-9787-8 (sc)
ISBN: 978-1-4808-9788-5 (hc)
ISBN: 978-1-4808-9786-1 (e)

Print information available on the last page.

Archway Publishing rev. date: 12/15/2020

I wake myself up, all ready for the day.

"Hello Planet Earth, happy to see you today!"

My name is Keke and I love my family:
My Mom,
My Dad,
My big brother, Noah.
And Clyde our dog whom my Mama calls "unruly."

Here's a picture I drew of them.

We live in an apartment that reaches high into the sky.

My family and I go out for
fro-yo smoothies.

I love to go to the library
for story time.

And we take Clyde
to the dog park.

Whenever we go down the elevator,
I give my neighbor friends one
of my Keke Super-Strong Double
Hugs. It warms everyone up and
makes us all happy.

Mama says we are always on the go.
Dad says that's what he loves about the city.
"Can we go for a walk?" I ask.

"Yes, let's go!" smiles Mama.
"I dig it, let's do it…" sings Dad.
"I'm cool with that," says Noah.

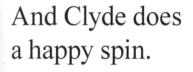

And Clyde does
a happy spin.

Can we watch Noah at the skateboard park?
"Yes, let's go!" smiles Mama.
"I dig it, let's do it…" sings Dad.

"I'm cool
with that,"
says Noah.

My Grandmas live together in a Retirement Home.
It's fun to visit them.

"Can we go see the Grandmas and play ping pong?" I ask.
"Yes, let's go!" smiles Mama.
"I dig it, let's do it…" sings Dad.
"I'm cool with that," says Noah.

The Grandmas love me and I love them.

But then, one day we couldn't go outside.
Anywhere.

"Can we go out for fro-yo?
Can we go to the library?
Can we shoot pool with
the Grandmas?"
But the answer is always No.

Clyde does not do a happy spin.

Mama says there is a
pandemic here now.
But what is that?
Where did it come from?
Why does it make
people sad?
Why don't I see it?

I don't see anything
different outside
except people are
wearing masks.

Will the pandemic come and get me, too?

Daddy says we have to stay inside more because lots of people are getting sick and some are even dying. When lots of people get sick at the same time it is called a pandemic.

Daddy says it comes from a virus like a cold, only this makes you much sicker than a cold.

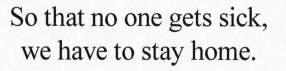

So that no one gets sick, we have to stay home.

Everyone seems frightened.

That makes me
feel scared, too.

The Pandemic feels big.
Everyone is worried or sad.
We can't go to any of the places I love to visit and
we can't even go in the elevator with our friends.

I can't give any Keke Super-Strong Double Hugs.
Not even to the Grandmas.

The pandemic stays and stays.
Some days I feel angry
             and I don't know why.

The pandemic is all we do.

But one day I have an idea.
"Hey," I say. "Let's make our own ice cream.
                    I choose triple berry flavor!"

"Yes, let's go!" smiles Mama.
"I dig it, let's do it…" sings Dad.
"I'm cool with that," says Noah.

"Hey," I say.
   Let's have story hour at home!"

"Yes, let's go!"
smiles Mama.
"I dig it, let's do it…"
sings Dad.
"I'm cool with that,"
says Noah.

"Hey," I say.
"Let's run Clyde inside our building
         so we all get exercise!"

        "Yes, let's go!"
        smiles Mama.
        "I dig it, let's do it…"
        sings Dad.
        "I'm cool with that,
says Noah.

"What if we have a special face-to-face computer call
with the Grandmas?"

"Yes, let's go!" smiles Mama.
"I dig it, let's do it…" sings Dad.
"I'm cool with that," says Noah.

We love
you all!
Take good
care!

We are safe.
You be careful
and safe too,
and wash your
hands for 20
seconds!

The Grandmas love us even when we are not together.

Every night Mama and Dad tell me they love me
and that they will always take care of me.

"And if we can't take care of you, Noah, the Grandmas
and other family will help. We love you very much."

"But what happens if we all get sick?" I ask.

"We are doing everything we can to keep healthy," says Dad.

"We stay inside and wear a mask over our
nose and mouth when we go out."

"We wash our hands with soap and warm water
to make the germs slide away," adds Mama.

"And if you did get sick, your doctor would
be there to help you feel better."

I love my family.
My Mama and Dad are
strong and brave. And
I'm glad Noah and Clyde
are here, too. And even
though I can't visit the
Grandmas they are safe
and they love me, too.

We take care of each other and that
makes me feel safer and better.

I draw a picture of my family being safe, even Clyde.

"Hey!" I say. "Can we have a family-sized Keke Super-Strong Double Hug to warm us up?" I ask before bed.

"Yes, let's go!" smiles Mama. "I dig it, let's do it…" sings Dad. "I'm cool with that," says Noah.

And Clyde does a happy spin.

"Good night Planet Earth," I say.
"Stay safe all around the world."

TALKING TO CHILDREN

The pandemic is hard for all of us to understand. This is especially true for young children who view themselves as the center of the world. Children can become anxious, clinging, and sad when their routines and creativity are disrupted. Keke experiences all these feelings and thoughts. Here are some suggestions about how to help your children:

- Ask your children about their thoughts and questions. This will help you find ways to talk about what feels different or scary.
- Give your children time to ask their questions. Reassure children that you will always answer their questions.
- Answer your child's questions with straightforward, simple answers. When children want more information, they will ask for it. Overloading children can frighten them and confuse them.
- Young children often ask the same question over and over. It is their way of learning.
- Respond to their thoughts by telling them, "It is very confusing. Let's think about it together." This helps children know you want to find ways for them to understand their "new world."
- Tell children that you will always keep them safe. They need this reassurance, so they don't become overwhelmed and frightened.
- Reassure your children that if you are unable to take care of them, then someone else they love will keep them safe.
- Explain to children that many people are trying hard to help everyone who is sick with the virus.
- Teach your children how to take care of themselves. Talk with them about washing hands, wearing masks, and staying away from other people not living in their house.
- Keeping a routine can help children feel less confused. Adding new activities to their routine lets them feel creative and adventuresome.

The following resource page has activities for your children, ways to talk with them, and ways to help yourself.

PARENT RESOURCES

Centers for Disease Control and Prevention (CDC)
(cdc.gov/coronavirus/2019-ncov/daily-life-coping/talking-with-children.html)
Talking with Children about Coronavirus Disease 2019

Center on the Developing Child, Harvard University
(https://developingchild.harvard.edu)
How to Support Children (and Yourself) During the COVID-19 Outbreak

The Children's Psychological Health Center
(www.childrenspsychologicalhealthcenter.org)
My Pandemic Story

New York Times (nyti.ms/3b8kU9q)
Children May Be Afraid of Masks. Here's How to Help.

PBS (www.npr.org/sections/goatsandsoda/2020/02/28/809580453/
just-for-kids-a-comic-exploring-the-new-coronavirus)
Just For Kids: A Comic Exploring the New Coronavirus

Science podcast Tumble (http://www.sciencepodcastforkids)

Scholastic and Yale Child Study Center (download in Spanish or English)
medicine.yale.edu/childstudy/scholasticcollab/resources-covid/first-aid-feelings/
*First Aid for Feelings A Workbook to Help Kids Cope During the
Coronavirus Pandemic*

Sesame Street (SesameSreet.org/HealthEmergencies)
Talking to Children about Covid-19

WTTW (www.pbs.org/parents/thrive/parenting-during-coronavirus-you-are-enough)
Parenting During Coronavirus: You Are Enough

ABOUT THE AUTHORS

Elizabeth McChesney has been a children's librarian for more than thirty years and worked as the citywide director of Children's Services and Family Engagement for the Chicago Public Library. She now serves the Laundry Cares Foundation and is a Senior Advisor to the Urban Libraries Council. She is the co-author of two professional books and has taught children's literature at Dominican University.

Judy Schiffman has worked with children for forty years as a teacher, therapist and administrator. Since 2008, she has been director of children's grief services at the Chicago Psychoanalytic Institute. She has taught child development and counseling in the Department of Psychiatry and Behavioral Sciences at Northwestern University Medical Center.

ABOUT THE ILLUSTRATOR

Steve Musgrave has worked as an illustrator in Chicago since 1979. His clients include the Chicago Public Library, the Lincoln Park Zoo and Lurie Children's Hospital. His art is also prominent throughout the City of Chicago.

CPSIA information can be obtained
at www.ICGtesting.com
Printed in the USA
LVHW071633030221
678276LV00017B/618